TOOT!

Taro Gomi

William Morrow And Company, Inc. New York

Albert had a trumpet. It went *toot*.
When Albert had the flu, he couldn't play his trumpet.
He had to stay in bed.

When Albert got well and went out to play,
he took his trumpet with him.

But when Albert blew, all he got was *blat.*

"What's that?"

When Albert blew again, he got . . .

Blat! Blat!

"A trumpet is not
supposed to do that."

But when Albert blew, he knew . . .

Blat! Blachoo!

The trumpet had caught his flu.

The doctor knew just what to do.

Albert put his trumpet to bed.
"Feel better," he said.

"Sleep well."

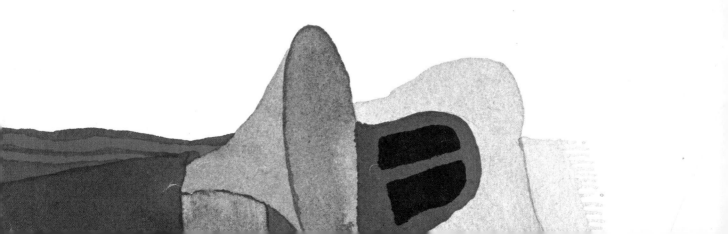

Good as new!

Toot!

TARO.

Copyright © 1979 by Taro Gomi

First published in Japan by Kosei Publishing Company under the title *Rappa O Narase*.

Printed in the United States of America.   1 2 3 4 5 6 7 8 9 10

Library of Congress Cataloging-in-Publication Data

Gomi, Taro. Toot! Translation of Rappa o narase. Summary: When Albert's trumpet catches the flu, Albert knows just what to do to make it well again. [1. Trumpet—Fiction. 2. Sick—Fiction]   I. Title.
PZ7.G586To   1986   [E]   85-32092
ISBN 0-688-06420-5   ISBN 0-688-0641-3 (Lib. bdg.)